IES 183375
s/6

the Pole

WITHDRAWN
FROM STOCK

CHRIS a ...

Illustrated by
JOANNA CAREY

HEINEMANN · LONDON

For Lorel, because he's up there, somewhere.

First published in Great Britain 1994
by Heinemann Young Books
an imprint of Egmont Children's Books Limited
Michelin House
81 Fulham Road
London SW3 6RB

Reprinted 1998.

Text copyright © Chris d'Lacey 1994
illustrations copyright © Joanna Carey 1994
ISBN 0 434 96801 3

A CIP catalogue record for this book is
available at the British Library.

Printed in Italy by Olivotto.

A school pack of BANANA BOOKS 67-72 is
available from Heinemann Library
ISBN 0 435 00098 5

Chapter 1

'YOU'D LIKE TO do *what?*' Miss
Harrison said.

Billy Cockcroft gulped like a giant
goldfish. All afternoon he had been
itching to tell his secret and now he'd
told it, he just felt daft. All his
classmates were gawping in
amazement. Billy shifted his feet and
said once more:

'I want to walk to the North Pole,
Miss.'

'Well, that's jolly interesting,' Miss Harrison said. And that made everyone *really* gawp. 'But why, Billy? What do you want to go there for?'

Billy looked around at his puzzled classmates. He had always wanted to go to the Pole. Ever since his dad had said...

'Yes,' coaxed Miss Harrison.

Billy took a breath and let the story tumble out: 'My dad says there's a hole in the sky there, Miss. If it gets too big the sun will come through and melt all the ice at the North Pole, Miss. Then we'll all be flooded. And worse than that, the polar bears will drown...'

There was a titter of laughter from the back of the class.

'I see,' said Miss Harrison. 'And supposing you were able to go on this trek, what would you propose to do about the hole?'

Billy swallowed hard and looked again at his classmates. He could see their cheeks puffed up like balloons.

'Mend it, Miss. I want to mend the hole.'

'Mend it?'

The class became a riot of laughter.

Children were hooting and falling off their seats. "Silly Billy Cockcroft," he could hear them shrieking. "He wants to be a hole-at-the-Pole mender!"

But Miss Harrison wasn't laughing. She was chalking up several large words on the blackboard:

Arctic
Polar bear
Global
Warming

'Now,' she said loudly, clapping the dusty chalk off her hands, 'this weekend I want everyone to find out what they can about these things. We'll do a project on the hole at the Pole.'

Chapter 2

'THAT'S A BIT of a tall order, isn't it?' Billy's mother put a plateful of fish fingers and chips on the table and Billy and his father began to dig in.

'Do a project on the hole at the Pole? All by himself! He's only eight!'

'Nonsense,' said his father, blobbing ketchup all over his fish fingers, 'he's a bright enough lad. Besides, he's got me to help him out.'

'You're the one who helped him *in*,' said Billy's mother. 'All this talk about

5

trekking to the Pole. He gets lost if he goes to the bottom of the garden.'

'Oh Mu-um,' protested Billy.

'Oh nothing,' said Billy's mum.

'Is there any bread?' said Billy's dad.

Mrs Cockcroft sighed and walked over to the bread bin. 'Well you'd better make a start after tea,' she said to Billy. 'It's no good leaving it till last thing on Sunday evening.'

'First I'm going to ask Mr Gribble for his stepladder,' Billy said.

Mr Gribble was the Cockcrofts' next door neighbour.

'And for the biggest flag he's got.' He also had a tall white flagpole in his garden.

Billy's dad groaned and covered his face.

'Ladders? Flag?' Mrs Cockcroft turned. 'What have you been telling him?' she asked Billy's father. Mr Cockcroft blushed as red as his ketchup. He often teased Billy and told him tall stories. This time he had been caught out.

Billy went on: 'Explorers always take a flag to the Pole, Mum. They stick it in the ice when they arrive. Dad said if we climbed up high on some ladders, we could spread the flag right over the hole and stop the sun coming in to melt the ice!'

'Enough!' cried Mrs Cockcroft. She

rapped her knuckles on the edge of the table. The end fell off Mr Cockcroft's fish finger. 'Never have I heard such nonsense,' she muttered. 'What you need, Billy Cockcroft, is a book about the Arctic.'

'Josie's got a book with pictures, Mum. She's coming round tomorrow to show it to me.' Josie Westacott was Billy's best friend. She lived in the house that backed on to Billy's garden.

'Good,' said his mother.

And that was that. The Cockcrofts settled in silence to finish their tea.

They were so silent, in fact, that none of them noticed something happening outside.

The weather was changing. The sky was turning grey.

It was well into April.

And it was starting to snow...

Chapter 3

'WOW!' CRIED BILLY, 'look at it, Dad!'

Mr Cockcroft stood on the doorstep the next morning, shivering. The tiny back garden was covered from the dustbin to the shed in deep snow. The only signs of life were the top few spikes of a conifer bush. There was even a drift against the hole in the fence that led into Josie's garden.

'Now we can practise our trek, can't we, Dad? We'll be like real explorers.'

Billy was stomping up the snowy lawn. He wore an anorak zipped up to his chin and a bright yellow bobble hat. His jeans were tucked into his wellington boots, which could barely be seen above the top of the snow.

'Err... I think we'll give exploring a miss,' said Mr Cockcroft.

11

'Aww, Dad!' said Billy. 'What about the Pole?'

Mr Cockcroft bit his lip. 'First things first. You should get used to the icy cold before we go exploring.'

He took a step backwards into the kitchen.

'Where are you going, Dad?' said Billy suspiciously.

'You practise for a while,' Mr Cockcroft said.

'What?' said Billy, making up a snowball.

'Survival training,' his father said.

Billy's snowball whizzed through the air.

It landed, *thud!* on the closed back door.

Alone in the garden, with a chill wind biting at his nose and cheeks, Billy decided he had better keep warm.

I'll build a snowman, he thought to himself. But as he scooped up the first big mound and started to roll it into a ball, he changed his mind. 'No,' he said firmly, 'I think I'll make something else instead...'

He was piling the snow into a really

huge mound when he heard noises in
the garden next door: the creak of
pulleys; the tightening of ropes. He
jumped up onto the garden bench, just
in time to see a red and white flag
being raised on Mr Gribble's pole.

'Morning, Mr Gribble!'

Mr Gribble stood to attention and
saluted the flag. Then he crunched
through the snow to the garden wall.

'Do you realise what day it is, boy?'
he said. He pointed at the flag and
waited for an answer.

'Saturday?' said Billy hopefully.

'St George's Day!' Mr Gribble boomed. 'And look at it! Look at the state of my garden!'

Billy stood on tip-toes for a better peek. 'It's been snowing,' he said.

'I can see that, boy. The point is, *why*? It's nearly May, so *why* is it snowing?'

Billy had an idea. 'It's because there's a hole at the North Pole,' he said.

'What?' said Mr Gribble. 'Don't be ridiculous.' Then he spotted the lump of snow in Billy's garden.

'What's that monstrosity?' he said unkindly.

'A polar bear, I hope,' said Billy.

'A polar bear?' Mr Gribble sneered. 'It looks like a giant boiled egg on legs.'

'That's because it hasn't got a head,' said a voice. It was Josie coming up the garden. She was dressed like Billy, in anorak and jeans. She smiled at Mr Gribble who frowned back.

'I need lots more snow for his head,' said Billy.

Mr Gribble peered slyly round his garden. A smile lit up the corners of his mouth. 'There's plenty here,' he said. 'Why don't you take some? Start with the path.'

Chapter 4

THAT AFTERNOON, BILLY and Josie worked
on their project. They sat in the kitchen
with their crayons and pads. They had
Josie's book spread open in front of
them. Billy was tracing a map of the
Arctic and Josie was drawing pictures of
animals.

Billy looked out of the kitchen window at his finished ice bear. The ice bear seemed to be looking right back. It looked so real that Billy thought it might be trying to tell him something. Something important. About the hole, perhaps? But that was silly. Ice bears didn't talk. Ice bears *couldn't* talk. He looked again.

Could they?

Josie's book said nothing about the hole - not where it was, or how big it was, and certainly not how to mend it. They had found a lot of other things good for the project – about the Arctic ocean and the Inuit people, but there was definitely no mention of any sort of hole. Billy felt disappointed. He wanted to know if the hole *could* be mended. He needed to tell Miss Harrison on Monday.

He was still thinking about it at
bedtime as he waited for his mum to
come and say goodnight. He was
rubbing his feet over the shaggy white
rug on the bedroom floor and thinking
that it looked like a polar bear's fur. He
told his mum as she came into the
room.

'I suppose it does a bit,' she admitted. 'Easier to hoover than a polar bear, though.'

Billy laughed. 'Mum,' he said, 'how far is one thousand miles?'

Mrs Cockcroft hummed. 'Oh, a long way. Why?'

'It says in Josie's book that the Arctic ice is wider than that.'

Mrs Cockcroft smiled. 'It's a big place,' she nodded.
'Mum. What does global warming mean?'

Mrs Cockcroft frowned. 'It's when the earth heats up – like having summer all the time.'

Billy thought hard. Ice melted in the summer. 'If we don't mend the hole and the ice melts, Mum, where will all that water go to?'

Mrs Cockcroft sighed. 'Into the ocean – where else, silly?' And she tucked him in and turned out the light.

Chapter 5

BILLY WAS TIRED, and asleep before he knew it. The last thing on his mind before he dozed off was one thousand miles of Arctic ice.

Soon he was dreaming – walking across the ice to the Pole.

In his dream there was nothing but ice as far as he could see. The wind was

whistling and the ice was creaking. It was freezing cold. He wished he had a hot water bottle with him.

Then in the distance he saw a shape – a flag, like Mr Gribble's, blowing in the wind.

The North Pole!

When Billy got close he saw a sign

that said: NORTH POLE HERE! There were other signs too. All of them were pointing away from the flag and most of them said: SOUTH – THIS WAY!

Billy looked across the shiny white ice and shivered. Just then he heard a thumping sound nearby. He thought he knew what that thumping was. He turned and saw a giant figure padding towards him.

The polar bear had a sort of swaggering walk. It had a big black nose and dark auburn eyes. As it lolloped forward, it swung its head upwards and sniffed at the air. Now and again it stuck out its tongue. Great puffs of polar breath blew from its jaws. Billy had never seen anything so beautiful or so frightening in his life.

He stood absolutely still, hoping the bear might somehow miss him. But when it was just a few feet away, the bear sat down, not unlike a cat. To Billy's amazement, it began to speak.

'Hmm, I thought it was you,' it said.

Billy stopped quaking. The great white bear seemed friendly enough. It also looked rather *familiar*. In fact, it looked like the bear in Billy's back garden. So Billy asked, 'Are you the bear I made?'

'Hmm... sort of,' the ice bear grunted.

'The other bears call me the Teller of Ways. I tell things, you see. Stories, mostly. You've come about the hole in the sky, I expect?'

'Yes,' said Billy. 'Do you know how to mend it? My dad says we need some ladders.'

The ice bear sniffed and trod the ice with his paws. 'Hmm,' it rumbled. 'I don't know much about ladders, but I do know the secret of mending the hole.'

'You do?' said Billy, excitedly. 'I've got to find out for Miss Harrison's project!'

'No doubt,' said the ice bear, looking bemused. It lifted a hind leg and scratched at its fur. 'Well, if you're keen to know about the hole, I can tell you the secret, but you have to make a promise.'

'Cross my heart!' Billy exclaimed.

'All right,' said the bear, and it padded closer. It snorted once and its breath smelt of fish. 'The secret is, the hole will mend itself – if enough people care to let it.'

Billy's jaw dropped. 'Is that all?' he said. 'We don't need Mr Gribble's flag?'

'I shouldn't think so,' said the bear. 'Have a look at this and then you'll understand.'

He took Billy to one side. Through the mists of the Arctic seascape, strange images began to appear. Pictures of Inuit and bears and ice, fading and tumbling through a hole in the sky. Round the edge of the hole was a funny, hissing cloud, a cloud that was eating the sky away and making the hole grow wider and bigger. But the strangest sight of all, when Billy looked closely, was that the cloud was full of the oddest things: old aerosols, fridges and fire extinguishers. It was these that were making the hissing sounds. They were leaking gases into the air; the gases were making the hole at the Pole!

Billy Cockcroft thought of his mum using her hair spray and his dad having a kick at the broken kitchen fridge. 'I promise not to tell anyone, honest!' he said.

'Er... mm... no,' said the bear. 'That's not quite what I meant. Please *tell everyone about the hole*. That's what I want you to promise. And tell them we've had enough of this stuff too...'

Suddenly a car went skidding by, blowing out a haze of murky fumes. Billy started to cough. So did the bear. Billy turned to see where the car had gone and could hardly believe his eyes. Now millions of cars were driving round the hole. They were making a layer of smog in the sky.

'Yuk!' said Billy.

'Absolutely,' said the bear. 'By the way, do you want to know another secret?'

Billy leaned closer.

'That smoky stuff is making it warm up here.'

Billy thought for a moment. It didn't

seem very warm to him. But he was pretty sure an ice bear wouldn't tell fibs. Quietly he asked, 'Is it true what dad says... that the ice might melt?'

'Yes,' said the bear, 'if nobody listens and the hole gets bigger.'

Billy swallowed hard and looked down at his feet. He wanted to help but he wasn't really sure how to. Then suddenly he had a wonderful idea. 'I know!' he whooped, 'me and Josie will do a drawing of the hole and Miss Harrison will know exactly what to do!'

The ice bear, known as the Teller of Ways, lifted his head and stared proudly at Billy. 'Come closer,' it said. 'Touch my fur...'

Billy walked towards the bear with his hands outstretched. He was scared but exhilarated too. Something strange was happening to the bear. His huge white

body was becoming transparent. Licks of icy fire were leaping off his fur. Billy closed his eyes and leant to touch the bear...

'Billy! What on earth are you doing down there?' Suddenly his mother was kneeling beside him. Billy was on the

floor. He had fallen out of bed. He was
flat on the rug stroking the shaggy
white wool.

The sun was blazing through the
opened curtains.

It was morning.

The dream about the ice bear was
over.

Chapter 6

MISS HARRISON *DID* know exactly what
to do. She got the children to make a
collage. The collage was so big, it nearly
covered a whole wall in the school hall.

All the parents came to see the
collage. Everyone said that it was
wonderful. So good, that the school
should start a campaign. *Mend the*

Hole at the Pole! they proclaimed.

And Miss Harrison said, 'Why not? We'll do it!'

Next day, a photograph of Billy's class, in front of the collage, appeared in the local paper. News spread far and wide after that – even as far as Buckingham Palace.

When the Prince of Wales came to visit the school, everyone cheered.

Billy was as pleased as punch. He had kept his promise and told everyone he knew about the hole at the Pole. Now the hole could start to mend because people *cared*.